THE OLDEN HOUSE

VINAYKUMAR

Contents

PROLOGUE

NOTIONPRESS PUBLISHING

I

THE OLDEN HOUSE

One's upon a time;There is a three friends. Two boys and one girl name is

rama

,kabir and prashanthi.They students are study in intermediate.Few days

After they intermediate is over.They students are passed-A1 grade.They can

Write eamcet exam.After one month eamcet result will be released.Students a

Qualified in exam.rama, kabir and prashanthi very happy.rama was planed

the tourist.kabir and prashanthi was Wow super idea.ok today night we can go.

They are finding the house.but they no any house.kabir seen the one house

The house name is olen house.There are relaxed some times.Persons stay in

the house.Because in the house there are all facilities.
rama ,kabir and prashanthi they are stay in the house 3 days.They very enjoy
In the house.In the house 2 days is left.rama and kabir was back in they own
house.What about prashanthi.where prashanthi.They have or not in the house.
Ook after few days letter.kabir and rama they confirmed the engineering seat
In the S.V college.In the college rama loving kavari.And also kabir loving
kavari.But kabir don't no rama love's kavari.And rama also don't no kabir
Love's kavari.But kavari really loving rama.Rama and kavari relationship 3
years in college.They completed his studies waiting for job.They are very
happy.Rama planed we can go tourist. Kavari say ok rama.The next day
they ready to tourist.rama and kavari was finding the living house.But they
No any house.Rama is thinking in past rama stay in the house.Rama tell
i know one house.The house name is THE OLDEN HOUSE.
Rama and kavari are lucky persons to stay in the house.Because in the house
there are all facilities.Rama and kavari are they completed her marriage.And
rama got job in hyderabad.
Rama is calling his best friend kabir.
Rama:hi
Kabir:hi !
Rama;how are you !

Kabir:iam fine raa

Rama:ok!how your job kabir

Kabir:ya!my job is good

Rama:ok

Kabir:your job nice or not

Rama:yes ya!good

Kabir:where are you ra

Rama:I am in olden house

Kabir:seriously! Why went yo there do know your flashback.

Rama:Has kk ra.I know ra you not

Serious kk na.

Kabir:Ha kk.

Rama:plz come here

Kabir:why!

Rama:you have pleasant surprise

Kabir:kk ra

Rama:bye

Kabir:bye I meet you

Bye

The next day kabir was came that olden house.rama is pick up the kabir rama

said kabir i married ra kavari.kabir is very feeling ook.rama and kavari are in

the house.kabir had kept the watchman to kavari.because rama habites.The

watchman is observing all in the house.Saying to kabir.rama and kavari they

don't no that watchman is watching in house.After few days kavari was

pregent.Rama and kavari is so happy.On that night rama,kabir are in bedroom

Kavari is in kitchen.The power was gone it is so dark one

shadow has went to

near windows.Rama was shocked he seen the near window.Kavari is came

near the rama.The next day rama and kavari went to hospital and kavari has a

8 month.In the hospital the doctor said that the baby is so healthy andient you

are getting a baby soon the doctor was said.Rama and kavari are felt is so

baby.kabir is helping to kavari in that time.

They came 9th month in pregnancy to kavari.The baby will be born on a his

daughter.Rama and kavari so happy.The daughter name is blessy.

One the day morning the blessy is in bedroom.The kavari is in kitchen.And

rama and kabir is went to camp for the hyderabad.In bedroom the biessy is

crying so loud.And kavari is not listening the crying.Kavari had went near the

blessy stopped the crying that seen of kavari.Near the window there is shadow

Kavari was saw the shadow and kavari was thinking that someone has in the

house.kavari is saw near the window they have ghost.she is shocked.suddenly

the sounds are came in the kitchen.

Kavari and blessy are went to near the kitchen and saw that two red colour

bangles.she was shocked seeing of bangles.kavari was sevaring and she is

tension.After sometime door bellis rang.kavariwent to near the door and opened the door.Rama and kabir was came house.

TO BE CONTINUED CHAPTER 2

II

Rama and kabir are in home.kavari want to tell about the bangles but the rama

was not listening.After some time rama and kabir are in the bedroom.kavari

was came to kept a dinner for rama and kabir.But kabir went to watchman ask

what you will observe watchman said that every friday,saturday rama was

going to camp that watchman is said to kabir.The next day friday rama went to

camp.kavari in bedroom.kabir went to near the kavari.

Kavari was shocked that kabir that why are you tension kabir.kavari was asked

to kabir.kabir saying to kavari.kavari rama is chatting you.Before you rama had

another girl friend.rama was killed that girl.5 years back rama killed that

prashanthi.The kabir had said to kavari.kavari is saying no rama is good

person.kavari went near kitchen and she was cooking .And kavari came to

near blessy and seeing there is some blood and red

bangles.Rama was eating.

Kavari near and asking that do byou have any friend in before our marriage.

She was died before our marriage she is best friend.my friend name is

prashanti.kavari asking about prashanthi.rama face is os tension.Rama went

to bedroom.Rama was did not ate dinner.kavari had confirmed that rama is

killed prashanthi.

Kavari was to know about prashanthi relation.kavari went to near kabir.but

kabir is full drink alcohol.kavari is back on his room.Went to near blessy.

Blessy had so fever kavari went to hospital.Rama in the house he is sleeping

Get up to sudduly.But kavari is not have.Rama is finding the kavari.Suddenly

kavari is came in front of rama was asked that kavari.where you going.kavari

Said blessy got full fever.Because iwent to hospital.Rama was watch that date

And time is 8'o clock and date is 12.Rama went to bedroom therewas a is

Prashanthi want to kill rama that date.kavari was went to kabir bedroom.kavari asked rama

flashback.

5 years back rama flash back

Rama,s college days.rama,kabir and prashanthi we are best friends.after my

eamcet exams over.rama planed tour.we are went to tourist came into the this house 3members stay in this house 3 days.In at 12 clock was killed prashanthi

Rama is loving prasanthi but prasanthi is loving anther boy.they getting

marriage soon.Rama was don't no prasanthi loving anther boy.

One day prasanthi was invited in this house party to prashanthi.In that party

Prashanthi boyfriend came.After party announced that.This boy is my

boyfriend.we are in love ana we are getting marriage soon.rama is shocked

and so anary on prasanthi.rama was went to near room in the middle of the

party.And after some time prashanthi went to rama room and asking what

happened rama.prashanthi said that what rama how is my twist.I know you

that you are loving me.But i am loving him.please don't disturb me and please

Continue our friendship.But rama was cetted me.Rama said kabir i want to kill

Prashanthi rama was decided rama is killed prashanthi.rama decided to killed

prashanthi.In the night time 8

date is 12o clock.After rama and me

We back to my home.javari is listen

the rama's flashback.kavari is crying. This rama flashback.

One's upon a time;There is a three friends. Two boys and one girl name is

rama

,kabir and prashanthi.They students are study in

intermediate.Few days

After they intermediate is over.They students are passed-A1 grade.They can

Write eamcet exam.After one month eamcet result will be released.Students a

Qualified in exam.rama, kabir and prashanthi very happy.rama was planed

the tourist.kabir and prashanthi was Wow super idea.ok today night we can go.

They are finding the house.but they no any house.kabir seen the one house

The house name is olen house.There are relaxed some times.Persons stay in

the house.Because in the house there are all facilities.

rama ,kabir and prashanthi they are stay in the house 3 days.They very enjoy

In the house.In the house 2 days is left.rama and kabir was back in they own

house.What about prashanthi.where prashanthi.They have or not in the house.

Ook after few days letter.kabir and rama they confirmed the engineering seat

In the S.V college.In the college rama loving kavari.And also kabir loving

kavari.But kabir don't no rama love's kavari.And rama also don't no kabir

Love's kavari.But kavari really loving rama.Rama and kavari relationship 3

years in college.They completed his studies waiting for job. They are very

happy.Rama planed we can go tourist. Kavari say ok rama.The next day

they ready to tourist.rama and kavari was finding the living house.But they

No any house.Rama is thinking in past rama stay in the house.Rama tell

i know one house.The house name is THE OLDEN HOUSE.

Rama and kavari are lucky persons to stay in the house.Because in the house

there are all facilities.Rama and kavari are they completed her marriage.And

rama got job in hyderabad.

Rama is calling his best friend kabir.

Rama:hi

Kabir:hi !

Rama;how are you !

Kabir:iam fine raa

Rama:ok!how your job kabir

Kabir:ya!my job is good

Rama:ok

Kabir:your job nice or not

Rama:yes ya!good

Kabir:where are you ra

Rama:I am in olden house

Kabir:seriously! Why went yo there do know your flashback.

Rama:Has kk ra.I know ra you not

Serious kk na.

Kabir:Ha kk.

Rama:plz come here

Kabir:why!

Rama:you have pleasant surprise

Kabir:kk ra

Rama:bye

Kabir:bye I meet you

Bye

The next day kabir was came that olden house.rama is pick up the kabir rama

said kabir i married ra kavari.kabir is very feeling ook.rama and kavari are in

the house.kabir had kept the watchman to kavari.because rama habites.The

watchman is observing all in the house.Saying to kabir.rama and kavari they

don't no that watchman is watching in house.After few days kavari was

pregent.Rama and kavari is so happy.On that night rama,kabir are in bedroom

Kavari is in kitchen.The power was gone it is so dark one shadow has went to

near windows.Rama was shocked he seen the near window.Kavari is came

near the rama.The next day rama and kavari went to hospital and kavari has a

8 month.In the hospital the doctor said that the baby is so healthy andient you

are getting a baby soon the doctor was said.Rama and kavari are felt is so

baby.kabir is helping to kavari in that time.

They came 9th month in pregnancy to kavari.The baby will be born on a his

daughter.Rama and kavari so happy.The daughter name is blessy.

One the day morning the blessy is in bedroom.The kavari is in kitchen.And

rama and kabir is went to camp for the hyderabad.In bedroom the biessy is

crying so loud.And kavari is not listening the crying.Kavari had went near the blessy stopped the crying that seen of kavari.Near the window there is shadow

Kavari was saw the shadow and kavari was thinking that someone has in the

house.kavari is saw near the window they have ghost.she is shocked.suddenly

the sounds are came in the kitchen.

Kavari and blessy are went to near the kitchen and saw that two red colour

bangles.she was shocked seeing of bangles.kavari was sevaring and she is

tension.After sometime door bellis rang.kavariwent to near the door and

opened the door.Rama and kabir was came house.

OFF STORY COMPLETED

Rama and kabir are in home.kavari want to tell about the bangles but the rama

was not listening.After some time rama and kabir are in the bedroom.kavari

was came to kept a dinner for rama and kabir.But kabir went to watchman ask

what you will observe watchman said that every friday,saturday rama was

going to camp that watchman is said to kabir.The next day friday rama went to

camp.kavari in bedroom.kabir went to near the kavari.

Kavari was shocked that kabir that why are you tension kabir.kavari was asked

to kabir.kabir saying to kavari.kavari rama is chatting you.Before you rama had

another girl friend.rama was killed that girl.5 years back rama killed that

prashanthi.The kabir had said to kavari.kavari is saying no

rama is good

person.kavari went near kitchen and she was cooking .And kavari came to

near blessy and seeing there is some blood and red bangles.Rama was eating.

Kavari near and asking that do byou have any friend in before our marriage.

She was died before our marriage she is best friend.my friend name is

prashanti.kavari asking about prashanthi.rama face is os tension.Rama went

to bedroom.Rama was did not ate dinner.kavari had confirmed that rama is

killed prashanthi.

Kavari was to know about prashanthi relation.kavari went to near kabir.but

kabir is full drink alcohol.kavari is back on his room.Went to near blessy.

Blessy had so fever kavari went to hospital.Rama in the house he is sleeping

Get up to sudduly.But kavari is not have.Rama is finding the kavari.Suddenly

kavari is came in front of rama was askcd that kavari.where you going.kavari

Said blessy got full fever.Because iwent to hospital.Rama was watch that date

And time is 8'o clock and date is 12.Rama went to bedroom therewas a is

Prashanthi want to kill rama that date.kavari was went to kabir bedroom.kavari

Asked rama flashback.

5 years back rama flash back

Rama,s college days.rama,kabir and prashanthi we are best

friends.after my

eamcet exams over.rama planed tour.we are went to tourist came into the this

house 3members stay in this house 3 days.In at 12 clock was killed prashanthi

Rama is loving prasanthi but prasanthi is loving anther boy.they getting

marriage soon.Rama was don't no prasanthi loving anther boy.

One day prasanthi was invited in this house party to prashanthi.In that party

Prashanthi boyfriend came.After party announced that.This boy is my

boyfriend.we are in love ana we are getting marriage soon.rama is shocked

and so anary on prasanthi.rama was went to near room in the middle of the

party.And after some time prashanthi went to rama room and asking what

happened rama.prashanthi said that what rama how is my twist.I know you

that you are loving me.But i am loving him.please don't disturb me and please

Continue our friendship.But rama was cetted me.Rama said kabir i want to kill

Prashanthi rama was decided rama is killed prashanthi.rama decided to killed

prashanthi.In the night time 8

date is 12o clock.After rama and me

We back to my home.javari is listen

the rama's flashback.kavari is crying. This rama flashback. After rama was came near kavari

near rama there is prashanthi kavari was saw prashanthi

and prashanthi his
ghost.prashanthi was killed by rama.kabir
Came near kavari and saying that about rama.rama is
chitted you also he went
to kill you and your daughter.kavari is in second pregnancy.
Kabir said that
again prashanthi was born on your stomach.kabir went to
is home.And kavari
also live that home and went to his parents in hyderabad.

THE END